To my husband, Scott,
and all the horses we've loved—
Bugs, Speedy, Mona, Rocky, and Coffee—
for they are the ones who lived this book.
—K.W.

To Leo Tremblay
—J.M.

The illustrations for this book were done in watercolor.
The text was set in HandySans, and the display type was hand-lettered.

 • Little, Brown and Company • Hachette Book Group • 237 Park Avenue, New York, NY 10017 • Visit our website at www.lb-kids.com • Little, Brown and Company is a division of Hachette Book Group, Inc. • The Little, Brown name and logo are trademarks of Hachette Book Group, Inc. • The publisher is not responsible for websites (or their content) that are not owned by the publisher. • First Edition: June 2012 • Library of Congress Cataloging-in-Publication Data • Wilson, Karma. • Horseplay / by Karma Wilson ; illustrated by Jim McMullan. — 1st ed. • p. cm. • Summary: A farmer tries to change the behavior of his rowdy horses, who play all night and sleep all day. • ISBN 978-0-316-93842-6 • [1. Stories in rhyme. 2. Horses—Fiction. 3. Farmers—Fiction. 4. Play—Fiction. 5. Humorous stories.] I. McMullan, Jim, 1936- ill. II. Title. • PZ8.3.W6976Hn 2012 • [E]—dc23 • 2011025120 • SC • 10 9 8 7 6 5 4 3 2 1 • Printed in China

HORSEPLAY!

By Karma Wilson

Illustrated by Jim McMullan

LB

LITTLE, BROWN AND COMPANY

New York ✶ Boston

One day while Farmer worked his fields
he cried, "For goodness' sake!
These horses are a worthless bunch—
they just can't stay awake."

And it was true: They snored out loud.
They slept the whole day long.
Farmer cried, "I'm mystified.
Something must be wrong!"

"Maybe they've been scared all night.
Have wolves been prowling free?
I haven't heard them howling,
but I'll watch tonight and see."

He spied from back behind the hay.
And what he saw was pure horseplay.

Those horses didn't sleep one bit.
They frolicked on the loose.

They joined in games like Hide-and-Seek,
Leapfrog, and Duck, Duck, Goose.

Donkey tried to play along,
but soon began to wail,
when all the horses gathered 'round
to play some Pin-the-Tail.

Farmer shouted, "I declare,
you horses have no sense!"
He shooed them back into the barn
and then padlocked their fence.

"I'm the boss, and what I say is absolutely

NO HORSEPLAY!"

But come next day the horses dozed.
They didn't work at all.
Farmer said, "Now what on earth?
I bolted shut their stall."

That night when Farmer locked them up,
he didn't go to sleep.
He snuck into the barn to spy,
and hid out with the sheep.

The horses shuffled decks of cards,
and passed out poker chips.
They handed out some veggie trays,
and seven-layer dips!

"So this is why
you snooze all day.
I thought I told you

NO
HORSEPLAY!"

He tied them up in separate pens.
"This silliness is done.
Now go to bed," the farmer said.
"And . . .

NO MORE HAVING FUN!"

But still those horses didn't work.
They acted just as lazy.
Farmer shouted, "There's no doubt
you're gonna drive me crazy!"

He hid out with the hens that night,
and watched as down below
his horses wrote out silly notes
and tossed them to and fro.

And so . . .

Farmer stomped. Farmer stormed.
Farmer yelled,
"THAT'S IT!"
Farmer ranted. Farmer raved.
Farmer threw a fit....

Farmer fussed. Farmer fumed.
Farmer said, "Okay,
you really want to horse around?
Go on, make my day!"

Farmer guarded. Farmer glared.
He stayed until first light.
And not one horse would dare to play;
they had to sleep all night.

Farmer shouted, "HIP-HOORAY!
I'VE PUT AN END TO ALL HORSEPLAY!"

The horses felt like colts again.
They walked with heads held high.
But Farmer's eyes were strangely red.
He sighed a sleepy sigh.

Farmer slumped down in the grass.
"I think I'll rest a spell.

I didn't sleep a wink last night,
And I don't feel too well."

zzzzzz

Before too long poor Farmer snored.
And while he slept all day,
his horses took their bridles off
and crept away to...

PLAY...

PLAY...
PLAY!!!